STRANGE WORLD

PHILIP BEGHO

Monarch Books

STRANGE WORLD

First Published 2004

copyright © **Philip Begho** 2004
All rights reserved

Enquiries should be addressed to:

monarch_books@yahoo.com
Tel: +234 8060069597

ISBN 978-37529-0-1

PUBLISHED BY MONARCH BOOKS
NIGERIA

CONTENTS

Strange World

Lady Strange

The blokes were making such a din. Regina kept trying to shush them up, not so that there would be less noise at Mero's Bar, but so that her own noise would be heard above theirs.

Regina loved a noisy argument as much as any of the men. Sometimes I thought it wasn't really about the argument. It was about the noise.

There's something about newsmen and noise. It's like noise charges them.

Noise energizes them. Makes them do their work better.

I can't stand noise. But then I'm not a newsman. I'm only a writer of ironies, who must sometimes hang out with noisy newsmen and reporters in order to do his work.

My eyes wandered up the wall, to the framed picture that hung above the drinks rack at the bar.

I always wondered about that picture. It was the picture of Christ, the risen Christ.

What was such a picture doing in a bar?

Some Monday, I resolved, when life was good and I was feeling clever, I would suspend snooping for ready-made stories and try to invent something intriguing around that picture.

The racket at the table pulled me down from my musings.

The bunch was talking – I mean yelling – about pastors. It seemed to be the in-thing these days to talk about pastors.

Oruna from the *Comet* laid Regina a punch in the eye. At least it looked like a punch in the eye from where I was sitting. It was that stinging.

But Oruna should have known better. Regina recovered immediately and came at him with guns blazing. From the two sides of her tongue. Oruna fell dead. He would be dead for another three minutes at least. That was all the time Regina needed to dominate the racket.

I glanced across the table to the second woman there.

She was about Regina's age. About twenty-five. Now that I come to think of it, she could actually have been thirty-five.

She looked very strange sitting so quietly in the midst of all the hubbub. Well, since I was sitting quietly like her, I imagine she thought I, too, looked strange. Especially since I was a bloke.

But it was not just the woman's quietness that made her look strange. There was something indefinable and ethereal about her. She was beautiful, but not in the way that made a man desire her.

I noticed that, like me, she had opted for no poison – of the smoking brand or the guzzling or swilling kind. But she wasn't nursing any fruit juice like I was. Instead she had a small bottle of table water before her, which she hadn't even taken a sip of.

Who was she?

None of the other guys had bothered to introduce her. I reflected that she might be one of the new lot the *Daily Times* had just recruited.

I could tell she knew I was staring at her. But there was no batting of the eyelids from this strange woman, from this Lady Strange; no flickering of eyelashes, no switching of her gaze to me.

She just looked on indifferently at Adubi who was now making the most noise, in spite of Regina's attempt to drown him with her raucous rattling.

God was visiting the news media, Adubi said, not quietly of course. That was why pastors were being employed by the dozen at media houses. He asked Timbala if he hadn't heard that two of the newly employed newsmen at *Daily Times* were pastors.

Timbala chuckled and said Adubi didn't have to go all the way to Agidingbi if he wanted to prove his point about pastors and the media. He, Timbala, seated at the table, seated right there in front of Adubi, was a pastor.

There was a hush. Beer tankards making their inebriate way to guzzly lips froze in mid-air.

"You are *what?*"

Timbala narrowed his eyes and took a long draw on his cigarette. "I'm a pastor." He drew an ashtray near and coaxed his cigarette to an elegant perch, then took a long guzzle from his tankard.

The table burst into laughter. Everyone laughed except Lady Strange.

And Timbala.

Timbala wiped his lips with the back of his hand. "That's exactly the point I'm trying to make. You think because I smoke and drink I can't be a pastor. Why can't I be a pastor when even angels smoke and drink?"

"Do angels smoke and drink?" That was Regina, her eyes freaking in alcoholic squint.

"Don't you know that Hell is filled with smoke and liquid fire?" asked Tunji Tade of *Thisday*. "It must be all the cigarettes and *kain-kain* they have there."

Timbala cast a stony eye on Tade. "I'm not

talking about fallen angels. I'm talking about divine beings." He drew on his cigarette. "You see, it's all about logic. Today's pastors have made sacred things look common. They talk about seeing angels here and seeing angels there. Angels wear suits and T-shirts and agbadas. They are in bars and marketplaces. They have become common. They are like ordinary men."

"So what's the logic?" asked Austin Akiji of *Vanguard*.

Timbala downed a frothy quaff. "It's simple. Since angels have become like ordinary men, they'll soon be smoking and drinking like ordinary men."

There was silence for a moment, then Mayaki of the *Guardian* began to chuckle. "I actually thought you had caught an angel smoking and drinking."

"We must stop them," insisted Timbala, suddenly jettisoning his put-on cool.

"What's wrong anyway if angels want to smoke and drink?" asked Regina. She had such a sweet, deceptively concerned look on her face that we all couldn't help laughing.

"Be serious, guys!" Timbala spumed, cutting our laughter short. "We really can't have these pastors making sacred things look common. We've got to stop them!"

Adubi protested that if Timbala wanted to stop anyone, it would have to be God. Because it wasn't the pastors sending angels all over the place, but God.

Timbala erupted. "Are you saying you believe angels are actually appearing in our midst?"

Oruna, awaking from the dead, rose to his feet. "Are you saying you actually believe angels exist?"

"*That* I think, *is* the real question," said Austin Akiji.

"No, no, no!" yelled Regina. "The *real* question is, why are you guys such chauvinists? Why are you talking of angels wearing suits and T-shirts and agbadas and not frocks and skirts?"

For the next seven and a half centuries – I really didn't look at my watch, but it must have been that long – the argument raged around the gender of angels. Then Austin deftly brought it back again to whether angels existed at all.

I shifted in my seat, preparing to rise and leave. This loud and curious tribe, I mused, had only noise for me today, no curious story, no irony.

"Not everything is what we think it is!" yelled Mayaki. He wasn't yelling just to the noisy table but to the whole of Mero's Bar.

I suppose he meant that when we think we have seen an angel, we might not really have seen one. Whatever he meant, I really didn't care. I would go elsewhere in search of my short story.

I rose to my feet.

There was a clearing of the throat. It was Lady Strange.

I sat right down again. If Lady Strange had at last chosen to break her vow of silence, you could bet I'd be all ears.

"I do believe Mayaki has a point there," she said.

Her voice was like the music of castanets floating in water; like the music I heard on a sandy beach under coconut palms in a dream I had many years ago when life was young and beautiful and my head was filled with sweet and lovely things and I lived the care-free life of a bohemian.

"Not everything is what we think it is," she repeated. There was a glint in her eyes. It was obvious she was going to launch into a story. We all shifted in our seats to make ourselves more comfortable.

I found myself thinking how strange it was that every one of the bunch suddenly went quiet when Lady Strange cleared her throat to speak. The sound she had made was a delicate, subtle one, yet the whole raucous lot had been stilled by its power.

Now, as we waited for her story, we were all hugging our seats, our ears throbbing like satellite dishes starved an aeon of signals.

"I remember Elsie," Lady Strange said. "Elsie was Goody Nelson's wife. You remember Goody Nelson of the *Clarion*? Elsie, his wife, had a rather odd experience one night."

Lady Strange smiled. "Not everything is what we think it is." Her eyes traveled slowly to each one of us, then when she seemed satisfied that she had caught our attention, she launched into the story of what happened to Elsie Nelson.

***

Deep in the night Elsie Nelson turned and raised herself slightly from the bed with her elbows.

She had heard something. She was sure of it. There was something somewhere in the dark.

Something...

She listened for a chuckling, an odd chuckling, a weird and eerie chuckling sound she was sure she had heard, but there was only the quiet of darkness now, the sound of silence.

Silence...

She lay still, listening, Goody asleep by her side.

Then she heard it.

Someone was laughing. Someone was laughing somewhere in the house.

She knew it wasn't Junior. It wasn't Junior her son.

She looked across at Goody, her heart

thudding. About ten minutes ago when she had first heard the sound and had awoken him, he had said it was just her imagination.

Nevertheless he had got up to investigate, but had returned without finding anything amiss. Junior was sound asleep in his room. Everything was fine.

He was cross as crocodiles when he laid his head back on the pillow. He had a very busy schedule the next day, he reminded Elsie, and sorely needed his sleep.

Elsie scratched her neck. Should she wake him now? Surely someone had laughed somewhere in the house. And it wasn't Junior. *And it wasn't her imagination.*

Or was it? Was it her imagination?

She listened, her heart doing something of a rumba in double time.

A long moment of bated breath, then she heard it. Someone was laughing. *She heard it!*

It was a soft, gentle laugh, rolling like a murmurous brook, but there was something sinister beneath the softness. It was like the soft laugh of a cat. A cat amused by its shadow.

A cat?

Do cats laugh?

Elsie shuddered. This was silly. It had to be her imagination. Goody was right. It was her imagination. *It had to be!*

It was dark. Dark! Pitch black. No light. Not even a bedside light. NEPA had struck.

And somewhere in the house a cat was laughing.

No!

It couldn't be.

It was her imagination.

Yes, it was her imagination.

Elsie sighed and lay back on the bed. She had to try and sleep. Morning was too far away to stay awake the rest of the night. She had to try and sleep.

Drawing the sheets up to her chin, she turned on her side. Goody was sleeping so peacefully. If only she could sink into deep slumber like him and forget everything, all this silly nonsense. She had only been imagining things. All was safe. Safe as houses.

Elsie closed her eyes.

Then bolted right up. *There again! She had heard it! She had heard it! Someone was laughing! She had heard it!*

The laughing was a bit different this time. It was like the chuckle one would make at a funny thought that crossed one's mind.

Someone was amused at a passing thought.

Someone weird…

…was amused at something weird.

In her house…

At night.

Elsie drew herself against the headboard.

The laughing stopped.

"But I heard it," Elsie muttered under her breath. "I wasn't imagining anything. I heard it!"

Goody moaned softly in his sleep.

Elsie glanced at him. *Should I wake him?* she agonized. *But there's nothing to hear now. Only silence. He won't believe me.*

Then Elsie saw it.

And froze.

It was on the wall. A pair of eyes. Eyes like two narrow strips of light. Staring at her.

Eyes.

Strange eyes.

Like strips of light.

Strange.

Strange and terrifying...

All Elsie could think, as the eyes stared at her, was: *What do you want?*

The eyes blinked.

It can hear me! Elsie screamed silently. *The*

thing can read my mind!

Of course, it can hear you! Of course, it can read your mind! Of course, it knows what you're thinking! What did you think?

Elsie shivered. *I should wake Goody, but I can't move! I can't move!*

The eyes blinked.

It heard me! It heard me!

Of course, it heard you. So now what are you going to do?

Elsie stared at the eyes, fear gnawing away at her innards, her heart in a riot of thumping, her limbs tense and immobile. Tense and immobile when they should be a-frenzy to wake Goody up!

I'm dead, she thought.

The eyes blinked.

For a long moment the eyes stared at the woman who thought she was dead. They stared unblinking.

Stared unblinking.

Then the cat began to laugh away. The cat was laughing its soft weird laugh. And the eyes were blinking and blinking.

The eyes were blinking as the cat was laughing. But the cat was not in the room. It wasn't even in the house, Elsie now realized.

The cat was outside.

Outside.

Then the cat's laugh grew and became the sound of an engine. The engine of a car on the street outside. A car being kicked to life. A car finally responding properly to its ignition.

The car moved, and the eyes, the two strips of light that had terrorized Elsie, rode along the wall and then vanished.

Vanished as the car took its headlamps elsewhere.

Elsie collapsed on the bed with a great groan.

She was thankful. Thankful to God. Not because the monster cat had turned out to be a car and not a monster, but because she had not woken Goody.

If she had woken Goody she would never have been able to live it down. He would have laughed at her all his life.

***

There was a chuckling at the table. "That was a good one," purred Regina.

"So you see that I agree with Mayaki," said Lady Strange. "Not everything is what we think it is."

The chuckling grew into unrestrained laughter as the blokes gave free vent to their amusement. Newsmen love stories. Sometimes I think they love stories more than I do.

When I had had my fill of laughter, I cleared my throat to speak.

"You *see,*" laughed Regina, "you've even

stimulated Caponté to use his tongue. The man wants to speak!"

The whole table broke into another bout of laughter. The guys know me. I don't speak much. Earning a living as a short-story writer is such a dicey piece of business that I can't afford to do much talking. Talking robs me of the energy I need to listen to find my story.

"What I just wanted to say," I told Lady Strange, forcing my way through all the laughter, "is that I really don't know what to say."

The table burst into fresh laughter.

"But I know I want to thank you for giving me the story I've been looking for." I looked beseechingly at her. "May I see you for more stories? Where do you work? Nobody bothered to say."

"That's because we don't know," murmured Austin Akiji.

All eyes were now on the lady. She had hit it good with the gang and everybody wanted to know her. This new reporter was obviously soon going to become the talk of news desks.

But how was it that no one knew where she worked?

A smile touched the lady's lips. She pointed at the wall. "That's who I work for."

We swiveled our gaze.

There on the wall, on the wall of Mero's Bar, hanging above the drinks rack was the framed picture, the picture that had been there ever since the place became a watering hole, the picture that had always intrigued me by being in a bar. The picture of Christ. The risen Christ.

I knew what I was going to see when I turned back to look at Lady Strange.

I knew I was going to see an empty seat.

The gang all gasped when they saw that her seat was empty.

It had been only a few seconds. Only a few seconds since our gaze moved from her to the picture hanging on the wall.

But a few seconds was more than enough for her kind.

The blokes have all changed. None of them argue any more about things they know little about. Not even Regina. She leaves frocks and skirts to be frocks and skirts and allows God to be God.

As for Timbala…

Timbala has left the *Morning Post.* He now works as a pastor, a full-time pastor, whose preaching throws much light on the ministry of angels.

Strange world.

Grain

The problem with Restaurant Albert was that excellent food was served there at too moderate a price.

In Accra they never use the word "cheap" for excellent food sold inexpensively. They say "moderate." Well, food sold at Restaurant Albert had far too moderate a price tag and so the restaurant was always crowded.

As I stood at the threshold of the restaurant I was in two minds: to invade some other restaurant of the splendid Volta Vogue hotel for a fine meal, as I had done in the last two nights, or, in this my last night, to brave this popular and crowded haunt of the Ghana media cream for not just a fine meal, but a most delicious and excellent dinner.

"Caponté!" I heard out of the hum of voices. "Caponté!"

It was a woman's voice.

I turned and saw my old friend Efua Anwuku beckoning me over from a corner table.

Seated by her was a distinguished-looking gentleman. I wondered if Efua had finally decided to give up her independence for the soft-sweet arms of wedlock.

I had not seen her since the assassination of Justice Minister Chief Bola Ige. She roved the West Africa sub-region as a senior correspondent for Reuters and had flown into Lagos to report the assassination.

"Hop in," she said, opening the door of a rented car, when we met at the *Vanguard* office at Kirikiri. "I'm on my way to Ibadan. I know you'd like to pay your condolences to the family."

We had gone to Ibadan, to the Ige residence, and I had paid my condolences and done all I knew to honor the slain icon.

But I couldn't say the same for Efua.

"How could you do such a thing?" I lashed out on our way back to Lagos.

"What?"

"How could you say that?"

"What did I say?"

"I heard you! You told Mama Ige that a grain of wheat must fall to the ground and die –"

"In order to live anew in the teeming sheaves the death of the grain births," Efua finished for

29

me.

"How could you say that?"

"I didn't only say that. I said Chief Bola Ige was no ordinary man, but a grain of wheat. And so he lives still."

"Yes, but it was all so insensitive!"

Efua had asked me how her condolence had been insensitive and I had stuttered for words.

The truth was that the whole matter of a grain of wheat dying confused me and I had never satisfactorily worked out its ramifications.

What meaning, I wondered, did the metaphor bring to the phenomenon of great lives prematurely truncated? Just how exactly did a grain of wheat, dying, live again, a greater life, in the real world around me?

Had good – much good – ever really come from martyrdom in a way that could be felt, could be seen?

The next time I was in touch with Efua was

when her twin brother, Kofi, got killed. Kofi was no ordinary twin but was the paragon of excellence to Efua.

"Next to God, it is Kofi," Efua always used to say.

Their love was legendary. Kofi Anwuku was a brilliant fellow who had bagged an Oxford degree, a triple first, in Politics, Philosophy and Economics, and had gone on to Harvard to take a degree in Law.

But Law was only intended to train Kofi's mind. He had no thoughts of practicing. When he returned to Ghana he went straight into politics – whatever politics there was that hadn't been totally garrotted by military interregnumcy.

His career was meteoric, and when democracy emerged, he emerged with it a presidential candidate.

And he was only thirty-five.

But Kofi's ambitions were stillborn. He fell

to the assassin's bullet, and the assassin was never found.

I hadn't seen Efua in the intervening time. But the news that reached me indicated that she had suffered greatly as a result of her brother's death.

"So, I don't have to go to Nigeria to see you," Efua laughed, as we hugged at the corner table of the Restaurant Albert.

I reminded Efua that we had a knack for running into each other at media hangouts in various capitals of the world, and didn't only meet in Nigeria.

Efua laughed. "Thank God for international conferences," she said. "I remember Beijing. And there was Kyoto, too. And Paris and Rio and Copenhagen. Those were good days!"

Something in her voice told me the "good days" referred to all that time before her beloved brother was cut down.

As though she read my mind she added with a smile, "But I have found peace, Caponté. You can see from my laughter that I have peace and joy again."

She introduced her companion as Pastor Yaw Yedru, founder of Christ Charity Ministries.

My meal had barely arrived when Efua had to dash off, summoned by her cell phone to news-gathering imperatives.

"You journalists are like doctors on call," Pastor Yedru remarked. "It's a wonder you ever get a meal down."

"I'm not a journalist," I replied. "I'm a writer."

I explained that though like the journalist I was often on the trail of happening events, it wasn't for the news story that I hunted, but for the short story.

"But newspapers find my stories quite suited to their readership. I'm syndicated."

"Oh, a syndicated writer. You must make pots of money."

"Not quite," I laughed. "But I get by. The great thing is that I like to travel and the newspapers have the idea that I can't write until I travel. So they pay my travel expenses."

"Accra should fetch you lots of stories. I bet you have a dozen tucked under your belt."

I shook my head. "I write a peculiar kind of short story. The *irony*. That's what newspaper readers seem to like. Unfortunately, ironies don't come in dozens. I haven't been able to find even one. And I have to return to Nigeria tomorrow."

Pastor Yaw Yedru did a strange thing. He abruptly placed his cutlery down and gave me a long, searching stare.

I felt very uncomfortable and was going to say something, anything, but he took his cutlery up again as if nothing had happened and ate his last forkful.

"Anything more, Pastor?" asked a hovering waiter.

Pastor Yedru placed several high denomination cedi notes on the table. "This should cover the three meals and give you a handsome tip," he told the waiter.

"Yes, sir!" the waiter said, whisking up the notes. His eyes gleamed as he gazed at the notes. "Yes, sir! God bless you, Pastor! I shall be in church tomorrow. Surely, I shall be in church. Thank you, sir! Thank you very much, sir!"

"You must excuse me," Pastor Yedru said, rising to his feet. He beamed down at me. "Will I see you in church tomorrow?"

"Me?"

I was bemused. Since when had I become a church person?

Yaw Yedru handed me his card, his grin broadening. "All the information you need is on the card," he said. "See you in church tomorrow." And he strode off.

I chuckled.

S*ee me in church?*

"You don't seem to understand, Mr Pastor, sir," I muttered, as I watched his back recede. "But I'm not the religious type. Besides, I've got a plane to catch tomorrow. Besides, I haven't yet got my story. Every minute I have will be spent trying to get my story."

I frowned. "Besides, do you think I'm bribable? Do you think by paying for my meal you can bribe me to come to church? Like you bribed the waiter? Like you *bribed* the waiter? *Like you bribed the waiter?*"

***

The next morning I put my bags in a taxi and headed for Kotoka International Airport.

"Happy Sunday, sir," the taxi-driver said into his rear-view mirror.

"I'm from Nigeria," I said.

"Is that?"

"In Nigeria we don't say things like 'Happy Sunday.' We say 'good morning' or something conventional like that. Not unless you choose to speak in direct Yoruba translation."

"Is that?"

"And we don't say 'Is that?' either. We say 'Is that so?'"

"Is that?" the taxi-driver said.

I hissed. I don't usually hiss. At least not so early in the morning. But this taxi-driver was annoying me. He should have seen that I was not in the best of moods.

When I hailed him and told him I needed to catch a nine o'clock flight, he had shaken his head and remarked that it would be pretty tough going.

Didn't I know?

I had overslept. Who wouldn't, crawling back to the Volta Vogue at 5 a.m. from everywhere but where my story was. Now the man was *is that*-ing me to a crawling pace.

"My good man, will you care to step on the gas?"

"My name is Kwesi, sir."

"Kwesi, step on the gas!"

"Why don't we stop at a church, sir?"

"Stop at a church? Are you off your rockers?"

"To catch your flight, you would need a miracle. Pastor Yedru is a miracle-worker. I recommend his church."

"*Yaw Yedru?*"

"His church is on the way."

"I met him only yesterday," I remarked, taken aback by the coincidence.

"His church is very close to the airport," Kwesi pressed. "Should I take you there, sir?"

Take me there?

This Kwesi was the most ludicrous fellow I

had ever met. "Will you move this crate, Kwesi," I snapped. "Move it!"

We drove in silence for several minutes.

"So he's a miracle-worker," I murmured. "Then why didn't he find me a story yesterday?" I was sore like mad that I was returning to Nigeria without a story.

"See this place?" Kwesi pointed to a huge, sprawling complex. "It's the Anwuku Youth Center. It was not built by the great Kofi Anwuku, mind you, but by Pastor Yaw Yedru. It's the greatest youth center in Africa. Young people have everything they need there. It has taken them off the streets."

"Is that?" I said, with a forced grin.

Kwesi evidently missed the joke. He went on earnestly, "Pastor Yedru has many centers like that, not only in Accra but all over Ghana. Youths, widows, motherless babies, the disabled, even those that need help upstairs – he has care centers for them, social centers. He has schools, hospitals, farms, bore holes..."

"Is that?" I was determined to make Kwesi see that I had eyes only for my flight back to Lagos.

But the man's grave earnestness was impregnable. "And all in less than two years, sir," he told me. "Less than two years! Is he not a great miracle-worker? He has done what no government can do."

"Where did he get the money from?" I queried.

"His church is very big and the people keep giving him money. But it is not just his church people. Everybody, including organizations – even organizations overseas. They have seen that the pastor does not chop money but uses it to help people. Do you know the pastor has only one car?"

I was going to say, "Is that?" but the cab

began to slow down the way cars do when there is a sudden engine fault.

"Kwesi, what's wrong with the car?" I was in something of a panic.

"I don't know, sir."

The cab came to a halt at the entrance of a huge church.

"You can't park here!" A man sprang to the car. His breast-apron was emblazoned with the legend *Christ Charity Ministries*. Needless to say we had come to the doorstep of Yaw Yedru's church.

"We are not parking," Kwesi told the traffic warden.

"No stopping at the entrance either. But I shall let you off this once. Come down quickly." And the warden opened my door.

"We're not here for the service," I snapped, shutting back my door. "This is a breakdown!"

It was only when the cab had been pushed

out of the way that I alighted.

"Find me another cab," I ordered Kwesi. "I must catch my flight."

Kwesi stopped three cabs in quick succession, but none agreed to convey me to the airport.

"They are looking for good money," the driver sighed, casting a glance at Kotoka International Airport, only seven minutes walk away.

I didn't have seven minutes. "Tell them I'll pay ten thousand cedis – anything!" I yelled at the poor obliging man. "I just must catch my flight!"

The roar of an aircraft taking off from the airport jerked us both round.

Sighting the colors of the aircraft, Kwesi threw me a glance. I turned away, crestfallen.

I had missed my flight.

***

Having secured a seat for the next flight, I left the Kotoka International Airport.

When on a Sunday morning in Accra you cannot find a story at the airport, and you need a story badly and don't want to stray too far from the airport, you are advised to go to a nearby church.

The bigger the church, the better. Stories are found with people, especially people given to great passions, and the greater the size of such an assembly of people, the better your chances of finding a story.

Thus it was that I found myself in the innards of Christ Charity Church. It was a huge church, jam-packed with all manner of people. And there were policemen around, too. Droves of them.

As I stood at the periphery of the crowd, jostled by those like me who couldn't find a seat,

I wondered what the blue boys were doing in church in such large numbers. Was the service a special service for the police?

At the pulpit was Yaw Yedru. It was him all right. Yaw Yedru. Looking immaculate in a white suit. An impeccable white suit.

What was this he was saying? It couldn't be. Was it Efua Anwuku he was talking about? Asking Efua to come up to give her testimony?

Since when did the Oxford-trained Efua begin to do this sort of thing? Begin to go to church and give testimonies?

It couldn't be Efua Anwuku, twin sister of the slain presidential candidate, the urbane and illustrious Kofi Anwuku. No, it couldn't be the Efua I knew.

A hand grasped at me.

Efua!

"Come along," Efua Anwuku insisted, gripping me tight.

"Efua! I never knew you were a church person!"

"I'm not. Only a Jesus person."

She took me right to the front row of seats.

"Enjoy the company of the police chief," she muttered, pointing me to a vacant seat by a resplendently uniformed gentleman who smiled benevolently at me.

So that's why the blue boys are all over the place, I mused. *Their boss is here.*

Efua had stepped up to the podium.

"The moment we've been waiting for," Pastor Yedru announced, handing the microphone to her.

Efua Anwuku wasted no time on preliminaries. "Success has many best friends," she intoned with oratorical deliberateness, casting a glance at Yedru. "But my friendship with Pastor Yaw is not at all the friendship of the fly and the honey-pot."

She paused. "When my inimitable brother was assassinated, my world came to an end. But I lived still. I lived only for one purpose: to kill the man who killed my silver Kofi. I bought a dagger. It was a silver dagger. I bought it to slay the man who slew my brother. I would kill him as soon as the police apprehended him. My heart was filled with such hatred – hatred that made me change my name to Efua Hate Anwuku.

"It was in the papers. I'm sure many of you remember. I was Efua Hate Anwuku. Then I met Yaw Yedru. He had just started his ministry and was relatively unknown. He wanted me to do some public relations work for him. I told him he was mad. Didn't he know I lived only to kill the man who killed my silver sibling?

"He said such hatred would only kill me. I said he was mad with a double portion. Didn't he know that I wanted nothing better than to die? Than to die after slaying the man who slew my brother?

"He said he would like to pray for me so that I could live long enough to kill the man who killed my brother. I didn't know what to make of this, and as I stood smoldering in my pot of puzzled hatred, he knelt down and began to pray for me.

"The relief that came as a result of his prayers was incredible – so incredible and so desirable – that after that day, whenever hatred swooped down on me, I would go to him to get prayed for.

"My hatred had indeed been strangling me, but whenever Yaw prayed, relief came. Relief came and I was thankful for it, but the relief was never long lasting. When Pastor Yaw and I got tired of its evanescence we embarked on a seven-day fast in the hope of obtaining permanent relief.

"I noticed that with each day of the fast my

hatred diminished. But guess what? It was replaced by depression. On the seventh day I was so depressed that I decided to end my life. I no longer hated the man who killed my brother, whoever he was. I no longer hated him, but if I couldn't kill him what was the point living?

"At eight o'clock that evening – I remember the day well – at eight o'clock I took out the silver dagger, and sitting at the edge of my bed, I put the point to my throat. I said a little prayer asking God to receive my soul.

"As I braced myself to plunge in the dagger, I heard a knock at the door. Before I could hide the dagger, the door opened and in walked a man I had never seen before. He was a man of stunning beauty.

"He gently took the dagger from my hand and said, 'A grain of wheat must fall to the ground and die, in order to live anew in the teeming sheaves the death of the grain births.'

"Those were the exact words that had issued from my lips in Lagos in so strange and curious a fashion two weeks before my brother died. When the man said that, his countenance changed and his beauty shone with the brightness of the sun. I fell at his feet crying, 'Lord!' And I worshiped.

"After a long moment, the Lord Jesus said to me, 'I have arrested your brother's killer.'"

"What? I couldn't believe this! Did Jesus just say he had arrested Kofi's killer?

"'I have arrested your brother's killer,' the Lord said. 'You have sought me diligently and have found me. Now know that I arrested your brother's killer months ago.

"'Know, too, that I have healed your emotions. The hatred is gone. Now by the act of your will you must forgive your brother's killer and tell him you have forgiven him. Only then will the grain of Kofi's wheat produce all the sheaves given to it.' There was silence. I looked up and saw that the Lord was gone.

"The next day I saw the killer, the killer the police had been looking for but couldn't find. I saw him. And I walked up to him. Yes, I walked up to the killer and looked him straight in the eye and said…"

Efua Anwuku paused. When she spoke again her voice was choked with emotion. "I walked up to him," she said, "and looked him straight in the eye and said, 'Yaw Yedru, I forgive you.'"

Efua Anwuku wiped a tear from her eye and stepped up to Pastor Yaw Yedru. I shifted in my seat as the two embraced.

Had I just heard what I thought I heard? Was this real? I looked around. The whole assembly was silent. Many people had their mouths wide open, as if it was the proper thing to do.

Pastor Yedru took the microphone. "It is all as Efua Anwuku has said," he told the congregation. "Before the Lord arrested me I was an assassin. A paid-killer. But after I killed Kofi Anwuku the Lord put an end to my work."

He looked around, then fixed his gaze on the police chief seated by my side.

"Now sir, you know why I took all the trouble to have you come," he told the cop. "I yield myself to the arm of the law and say let justice run its course."

You could have heard a pin drop as everyone watched to see what the police boss would do. The man's air of benevolence had suddenly been replaced by stern professional gravity.

He rose to his feet and strode to the podium. With him went dozens of gun-totting, handcuff-slinging officers.

At the podium, the arm of the police boss arched in a seizing swing.

But he didn't grab Yaw Yedru.

He seized the mike instead.

"The arm of the law," he proclaimed, "wilts always in the bosom of grace."

He swallowed. "I cannot speak for the Presidency or the Attorney-General's office, but I can speak for the police department. And I say this: What the Lord has arrested to produce stupendous sheaves of wheat, shall the police re-arrest to destroy?

"You all know the great works the Lord has wrought through the hand of this incredible man. You are all witnesses to the great sowing, the great harvest. Shall we destroy this?"

He stared at the congregation for a long moment, stared at his men, then walked away.

It is months after the event that I write this. News from Ghana says Pastor Yaw Yedru and his ministry grow stronger by the day. They are free of prosecutorial threats and continue their work, bringing succor and hope to tens of thousands.

What I find most fascinating is that troops of charity workers are being trained to replicate Yaw Yedru's work throughout Africa.

Once I was bewildered by the secret of the grain.

Once.

But no more.

No more.

All Things Work Together

I hadn't seen Tosan Tetsola for a long while. The last time I saw him was at the staff club of the University of Lagos, and that was at least four or five years ago.

I was having drinks with Professor Mudiamu and he popped in briefly and dashed out again.

The impression I had of this lecturer was of a fellow perennially on the in-dash and out-dash.

Tosan Tetsola was always frantically dashing in and out.

But it was a different Tosan that was by my side now, driving me to Asaba. A calm Tosan, a Tosan that seemed to have all the time in the world.

If I have to travel by road, I prefer not to go in my car but by those buses Nigerians call luxurious buses so that I can scribble a few things on the move. But I had arrived at Jibowu to see my bus leaving.

Tosan was fortuitously at the station, wanting to catch the same bus, but had missed it, not because his watch had gone slow like mine, but because he had been rather remiss about punctuality.

"Oh well, nothing for it but to take the car," he laughed.

We went to his residence at the Unilag campus nearby for his car and commenced our journey to Asaba.

As we left the Ikorodu Road toll gate, I grumped about my silly watch letting me down.

"All things work together for the good of those who love God," muttered Tosan, as he shifted gears.

"I wonder about that," I replied rather sourly.

Tosan chuckled. "I used to fret that way once upon a time."

I sat up. "Yes, you've changed. Really changed. What happened?"

Tosan laughed and then told me his story.

***

He dropped his spoon of rice. For the first time in two years of marriage, Tosan Tetsola had no appetite. It had nothing to do with Rowoli his wife, who was with him at table, or with her cooking.

As a matter of fact Tosan still considered Rowoli the best cook in the world and the best wife a man could have, but damn it, he couldn't lie, his frustration was strangling him!

"Rowoli, I really think I should quit!"

Rowoli glanced cannily at him. "You can't do that, honey. In what other job would you have the opportunity to be happily immersed in literature?"

"The only opportunity I've had," spewed Tosan bitterly, "is the opportunity of learning the names of all the *danfo* drivers from Akoka to Okokomaiko as I gallivant all over the city organizing seminars for the department. I'm just a glorified errand boy!"

Rowoli got up and went over to him. She squeezed herself onto his lap. She was like that. Always knew the right thing to do.

Tosan could not stop marveling that God had chosen to bestow him with such a wonderful woman.

"Don't worry, my darling," she said, stroking his cheek. "All the errand-boy stuff will end when your promotion comes."

True, Tosan reflected. But when would promotion come? When would he at last become a senior lecturer?

When would he be freed from the tidal wave of petty departmental errands – the lot of junior lecturers and the co-conspirator with the city's many exasperations to keep him from literature, his love?

And *how* would promotion come?

How?

Promotion in university faculties was based on research and the production of scholarly works. How could he produce even the sparest scholarly paper when he couldn't find time to make any visit to the boudoirs of literature?

All his time, yes, every bit of his time was

hitched to the mechanics of seminars and workshops and conferences. Even now he was exhausted from being the organizing backbone of a conference that was to be held in two days' time.

Administrative entanglements – that was the A to Z of his life!

Administrative entanglements upon entanglements! Their rabid tentacles asphyxiating all hope of contemplative work!

How could promotion come?

How?

That was Tosan Tetsola's dilemma, the heart of his frustration, the bones and very flesh of his perturbation.

And he as good as said this and more the next morning when he was summoned to the office of the Head of the English Department.

"Today is Wednesday," Professor Ogidan, the Head of Department, told him.

"I know that, sir," he replied.

"And you still haven't submitted any paper for the promotions board to consider on Friday? Don't you want to be promoted?"

"There's nothing in the world I'd like better than to be promoted," Tosan muttered, his tone barely disguising his bitterness.

"Why then haven't you submitted any paper?"

"I haven't written any."

Professor Ogidan laughed. "I was like that at your age – too shy to present any of the papers I had written. I never thought they were good enough. But I got cured of that silliness when I got tired of not being promoted."

"I'm not shy, sir," Tosan objected. "I just haven't had the time to write any paper."

The professor seemed to find this funny. He chuckled. "Okay, here's what we'll do. Rummage around in your drawers and fetch me any two or three drafts you find there. With a bit of assistance you should have something presentable for Friday. I know you're quite capable. What you need is confidence."

Tosan shook his head. "Sir, unless what you want is an old newspaper, I haven't as much as the first draft or scribble of a scholarly paper. I haven't written anything, sir."

The way Professor Ogidan stared at him now made it clear he was beginning to believe him.

"You have written nothing down – not even a rough draft?"

"I haven't had any time."

The HoD shook his head. "How an academic expects to make progress in his career writing nothing beats me."

"Sir, since I got on the faculty I haven't been able to read any substantial literature, much less put pen to paper. It's a wonder I've been able to teach at all. All I have is residual knowledge from my student days."

"And why, may I ask, is this so?"

"Why is this so? Pardon me, sir, but I'd have thought the answer was pretty obvious, seeing there is no end to the administrative errands I have to perform."

Professor Ogidan leaned forward. "Young man, we all had to do that as junior lecturers, but we made progress by not forgetting our primary assignment. We found time for study and research, Mr Tetsola, and whatever we did, we wrote. We found time for literature and wrote!"

A frown appeared on Tosan's brow. "Time is dead," he told the professor. "Slain in the streets by the city – by the monster the city has become. Slain by the rush and busyness of our times."

"Time never dies," the professor retorted, rising to his feet. "It's only men who die. Men without the will and resolve to subdue the city and milk time of its treasures."

Then why did you get up from your seat?
Tosan demanded silently, as his HoD started
pacing the office. *Is it because you knew your
statement was fraudulent in its idealism?*

Professor Ogidan turned to him abruptly.
"Write me *Literature in the City* for the
conference."

"What?"

"That's the paper Dr Sejojo was to deliver,
but he's backed out. Write it for me, Tosan
Tetsola."

"That's impossible, sir. The conference is
tomorrow!"

"Just give us a short and basic – even flimsy
– work that would rescue the department from
the disgrace of a back-out," the HoD pressed.

Flimsy?

Flimsy...

Flimsy didn't seem so impossible.

"And then present it on Friday to the

promotions board and you'll be promoted a senior lecturer."

"I'll be promoted a senior lecturer?"

"I guarantee it."

Tosan Tetsola needed no more convincing.

A few minutes later he was en route to pick the brains of Professor Ebere, now retired, who Ogidan told him had done similar work.

"The three or so hours you spend in this pursuit will be well worth the trouble," Ogidan had said.

As it was now Tosan had spent more than three hours in the Lagos traffic and was still a long way from the abode of the retired don.

The situation would be more tolerable, he thought, glancing at Soyinka's *Ake* on his lap, if I could only free my arms sufficiently to lift that book.

He had brought *Ake* along in the forlorn hope that literature had a place even on the move, but the sweating bodies that crowded his sides wedged his hands too tight to handle the book.

"Literature dies in the city streets," he thought wryly, "for want of arms to lift her up."

Someone in the bus gave a loud grunt.

Go-slow in the city was always awful, the person complained, but why was it this bad today?

"OPC is on the rampage," a fellow passenger offered.

"No, it isn't OPC," another countered. "It's those terrible *agberos*."

"No, it's the area boys!" another said. "There's a difference between *agberos* and area boys," he added inanely.

"No, it's the trade unions!" said another.

"It's the kill-and-go police!" a fifth person swore.

"No, it's university students!" a sixth man shouted.

No! No! No! It's the – it's the – it's the…

A babel of screeched speculations clashing with motor horns and the revving of standstill engines in a desperate, hopeless bid to strangle the cries of hawkers and pure-water kids – and the random yelling of the million, milling, wretched, weary, underemployed, jay-walking Lagosians who inhabit the entrails of the city.

Even were arms and hands supplied, would literature still live? Tosan wondered. *Can literature live in Bedlam's heartland?*

Tosan wrenched himself off the moribund bus. He needed to get away from all this. He would continue his journey on an *okada*.

Ordinarily he dreaded these demonic taxi-bikes, but could the risk they posed not be justified at such a time as this?

He had no choice.

No sooner had he zoomed off astride an *okada,* however, than he heard the screech of tortured tyres tearing through a tunnel of horrific cries.

A rude jolt forced its way up his shoulders and exploded in his ears in a deafening crash.

Was he dreaming? *He was flying through the air!*

THUD! He was in a ditch with garbage floating around him in stinking water!

Tosan gazed around the ditch in stunned dismay. Then he glanced at his soiled clothes.

"No! This didn't just happen to me!" he moaned with supreme indignation.

But his indignation quickly died when he clambered out of the ditch and discovered that the *okada* operator had been killed by the accident.

Dread seized him.

But dread was quickly replaced by the right emotion.

Thank you, Lord! he cried. *Thank you! I*

could have died like the okada rider, but I was spared. Thank you, Lord!

His bones creaked but none was broken; he had bruises but no major wound; *Ake* was mutilated beyond rescue, yes, and literature had died, yes, had died, but he was alive – alive and well.

Alive!

Much happened but Tosan was eventually taken by a compassionate onlooker to the backyard of a large, dilapidated building where he could wash his clothes.

He was alone when his clothes dried, and there being no side path round the building, he began to wend his way through the building's labyrinthine interior.

The corridor pulsated with strange machine-like sounds that kept the young lecturer wondering.

Going through a wrong door, he stumbled

into a large den bustling with men and machines.

Before him, cluttering the spaces between the men and the huge thumping machines, stood mountains of books.

Books and books and books!

Tosan stood dumbfounded.

He knew what he was seeing all right. The machines were presses – illegal printing presses churning out pirated books. The furtive ambience of hushed activity and the faded and shoddy covers of the books told it all.

As Tosan gaped, a woman dressed strangely in a man's agbada came in from one of the many doors that served the den.

"Emperor!" the workers hailed her. "Emperor!"

Perhaps they didn't know that the preferred form for her gender was "Empress," but Emperor she was, and Emperor railed away about some busybodies trying to spoil her business.

She swore they wouldn't surprise her as they had surprised Field-Marshall. She was much smarter than Field-Marshall. After all, she was Emperor.

As she spumed this last bit, she caught sight of Tosan.

"Who be *dat?*" she shrilled.

The workers, who in their busy furtiveness had not spared a thought for Tosan, now as a single snarling beast sprang towards him.

There is a time for argument and reason, and a time to turn oneself suitably footloose. Tosan opted for the latter.

But he hadn't gone more than a few paces when he ran into a wall.

A wall of charging men.

Men armed with truncheons and guns.

The book pirates chasing after Tosan all halted in their tracks.

One suspended moment!

One suspended moment then all hell broke lose!

Bellows and cries and threats!

Threats, threats, threats!

Threats to stand still or be fired at!

Threats!

Then the thwacks came. The thwacks of truncheons on bodies.

Thwack! Thwack! Thwack!

THUD!

The thud of bodies pummeled to the floor. Then the clanks. The clanks of handcuffs locking their jaws on defiant wrists.

What's happening?

What?

Tosan got his answer when he was shoved outside in handcuffs.

The building was besieged by uniformed policemen, and several patrol Jeeps revved around a Peugeot marked "Task Force on Copyright Violations and Piracy."

"What must I do to convince you I'm not a book pirate?" Tosan cried yet again as he was shoved into a cell at an *Isale-Eko* police station.

"I'm a law-abiding citizen of this country! A lecturer of literature! A custodian of books – not a pirate of them!"

If the police were deaf, not so Tosan's cell mates.

"Shut up!" they snarled as they began the customary cell bashing. "*Shut up!*"

A fist slammed home. Another.

Thus was Tosan's day hammered through rock-hard biceps into the knuckles of afternoon.

Evening was a thudding blow of hopelessness.

Night was worse.

It retched itself forth like vomit in its full regalia of discomfort. For though the cell-bashers rested, not so the mosquitoes.

Tosan had never seen such embodiments of greed as those *Isale-Eko* mosquitoes.

They drilled his blood with quenchless thirst, and when their little bodies were bloated drunken, they droned off to fetch jerry cans to secure more blood for the road.

But not even *Isale-Eko* police mosquitoes can stave off sleep summoned by the fatigue of anguish. Tosan's sleep was fitful but it brought relief to the knives of anguish.

Then morning came and woke him like a slap.

Thursday!

Thursday – the day of the conference!

What hope to still write the paper and receive promotion?

What hope?

Had God abandoned him?

He wasn't protesting when he refused the

breakfast that was tossed at him, it was just that he had no appetite for dung.

Lunch, too, was dung.

And time crawled through the entrails of pain to the bowels of deep afternoon.

Gone was what Tosan wanted most in the world.

Gone was his promotion.

His promotion was gone, but was he going to rot here? The police would not grant him access to a phone, would not let him make outside contact. What would happen to him? Would he die here?

"Tetsola!"

Tosan's head jerked round to see a policeman opening the cell door. But his eyes did not rest there. Behind the policeman was Rowoli.

Rowoli!

How did she find him?

It was in the taxi heading for their Surulere home that Rowoli answered this.

"Is there anywhere on the face of this earth you could be, my darling, and I would not find you?" she asked.

Tenderly she dabbed her handkerchief at the evidence on Tosan's face of the cell-bashing.

Tosan would have preferred the hanky at the corner of his eyes where the tears had begun to sting. What a wife he had! *What a wife!*

"When you didn't come home," Rowoli explained, "I spent the night going from one colleague of yours to another. I discovered that you were working on a paper and your last known destination was Professor Ebere's.

"After that I knew I would find you, even if it took the better part of the day – as it eventually did."

Tosan sighed. *What a wife he had! What a wife!*

They rode in silence for a bit, holding hands like the faithful lovers they were.

"I knew I had a very special woman for a wife," Tosan told his lady, "but gaining promotion and being free to indulge in literature was the most important thing in my life."

He turned and gazed deep in Rowoli's eyes. "Was the most important thing till I saw you at the cell door. Then I knew that next to God you were by far what I most wanted."

Rowoli didn't seem to hear.

"Mister," she called to the taxi-driver. "Change direction, please. Head for the University of Lagos."

Tosan stared at his wife.

What was she up to?

***

"In my pursuit of literature in the city, I barely escaped an *okada* death yesterday, was assaulted by the viciousness of book piracy, pummeled by frenzied policemen, chucked into a night cell and assailed to an inch of my life by cell-bashers and police mosquitoes... in the pursuit of literature."

The auditorium was wrapped in silence. The conference delegates, as a waiting coffin, exhaled no breath.

When Rowoli asked the taxi-driver to head for the university, she just wanted Tosan to do the noble thing, she said, of stopping at the conference to explain why there was to be no paper on *Literature in the City.*

"An explanation and apology in one word, darling," she had coaxed.

Swathed in rumpled clothes and stinging bruises, Tosan had hobbled to the podium with grudging acquiescence, thinking he would end up stammering out only a few words.

But now he could not stem the words.

The passion of frustration and pain, deep

within him, mingled with joy's sweet epiphany.

His was a joy and epiphany found only in that place where one has snatched life from death and discovered liberating truths about oneself. It gave terrible eloquence now to his speech.

Falling sometimes like the driving rain, sometimes like the soft morning dew, his words wove a marvelous tapestry through Tolstoic and Dickensian city conditions to Ekwensi's Lagos and Tosan Tetsola's own *Eko* – witnessed from the hard benches of *danfos* and *molues* and death-courting *okadas*.

Tosan spoke and spoke and then closed.

There was a hush. Then suddenly, a roar. The roar of thunderous applause.

Long.

Lingering.

Then the bustle of people coming forward to give more personal congratulations.

Rowoli was the first. She gave Tosan a kiss, full on his lips, his cell-bashed, swollen lips.

"Darling," she crooned. "Oh my darling…"

Professor Ogidan was next. A bear-hug of an embrace, then: "This is the finest paper on literature I've ever heard."

"Paper?"

"Since we must have it in black and white, I'll have it transcribed from the recorder, then you can present it to the promotions board tomorrow. But I can say this without fear of contradiction: you have your promotion."

Tosan Tetsola stared stupefied at Professor Ogidan.

When Rowoli had nudged him to the microphone to make his apologies, she had whispered encouragingly in his ear, "All things work together for the good of those who love God."

Turning, Tosan swept Rowoli up in the air.

"You were right, my darling," he cried. "You were right! All things work together! *Sweet Jesus!*"

And tears streamed from his eyes.

***

I looked out the window at the baobab trees that sped past us in the opposite direction.

Then I glanced at the watch that had failed me.

I glanced across at Tosan Tetsola.

There was a calm smile on his face. So he was now a senior lecturer? He looked so young, so boyish.

"You must be living it up now as a senior lecturer," I said.

"Actually I'm now a professor," he replied. "That's why I could take up residence on campus. Things happened quickly after the conference. Doors opened for me. Incredible doors of opportunity. Professors wanted to collaborate with me on one project or the other. There was so much goodwill."

He stole a glance at me. "Caponté, believe me, all things truly work together for the good of those who love God."

I was about to answer – I don't know what I was going to say – but I was about to answer when the heat and the sight hit us.

I don't know which struck first. The heat or the sight.

But there it was. The bus we had missed, on its back like a monstrous beetle.

Destroyed.

Destroyed for ever.

Passengers…

Passengers littered everywhere!

Dead. So dead. Burning. So burning.

Flames…

Mighty flames. Raging. So raging. So burning. So everywhere.

Death and burning everywhere!

No one survived the crash.

No one at all.

And I…

I kept the watch.

I still have the watch. The watch that ran slow. That failed me. That failed me and caused me to miss my bus. That failed me – and made me – in the hands of God.

I kept it.

Sometimes I wake up at night and hold it to my breast and say, *"All things work together for the good of those who love God, who are called according to His purpose."*

Who says men are not supposed to cry?

I cry.

Out of a Snake

They called him Snake. But no one seemed to know where to find him. I had a hunch that I would get my story if I could find him.

Warri was on the boil. Was it the Itsekiris and the Urhobos this time, or the Urhobos and Ijaws or what? The news hounds would find that out.

I wasn't a news hound. Just a syndicated short-story writer, and my editors in Lagos had sent me to the boiling oil burner for the simple reason that war or no war in Warri, life goes on in Lagos and people must have their stories and be entertained.

Humankind plays not with its stories. What is art but story, even visual art? What is a song but a story dancing on the wings of joy?

Even music – music without words – tells a story, the most enchanting kind, the dream kind, and not just any kind of dream, the kind everyone loves, the kind you point the beautiful way of your whim.

And so the story continues.

War or no war in Warri, life goes on in Lagos.

War or no war in Lagos, life goes on in Abuja.

War or no war in Darfur, life goes on in

Dallas.

If only men could see this. If only men would see that brothers don't really hate brothers but are tuned to acts of hatred and slaughter by a few clever men who do what they do for their own selfish ends, for their own power-hankering, pocket-burgeoning ends.

But men don't see this.

Men don't really see.

They see beer and *fufu* and girls to fool with. And public tills to dip their hands in.

And they see our stuff in the papers.

And we continue to write our stuff in the hope that one day in looking men would see. They would see what they should see.

I was looking today.

Looking to see Snake.

People said no one knew Warri and its woes like Snake. Some said he was Ijaw. Some said he was Itsekiri. Others said he was Urhobo.

They were divided.

Divided like Warri.

But they were united in one thing.

United as Warri should be.

They all said, all agreed, that Snake was at home with the Ijaw as he was with the Itsekiri and Urhobo, and his skilful diplomacy among the youths of the three warring groups had averted many a bloodbath.

Did people think Warri was a cauldron? It would have been an inferno but for Snake. His slithering tact bordered on the magical, they said. Bordered on the magical.

Snake.

I knew the man would have a story for me. Would have my story.

But where was I to find the man? Where was this Snake?

Perhaps Ernest would know, they said. Ernest was wise. He knew things. And you could trust him. That was vital. You could trust Ernest in this pot aboil where you didn't know whom to trust.

And so they took me to see Ernest.

He was in a dark and shuttered room at a meeting with some elders. I wondered what a youthful fellow like him could be discussing so earnestly with men old enough to be his father.

At first the elders swore at us for barging into their meeting, but their mood quickly changed when the spokesman of our little party explained that I was a correspondent associated with Reuters and CNN.

I usually make it a point to explain that though I'm syndicated in the newspapers, I'm not a journalist. But that sort of hair-splitting seemed rather imprudent in the stuffy little room now.

And the Reuters and CNN thing wasn't exactly a lie. After all, those chaps and I, in our search for materials around the world, often hang out in the same dives. And I'm on first name terms with quite a bunch of them, you know.

It didn't take too long, however, for the elders to realize that I wasn't interested in interviewing them but only in finding Snake, and their tempers growled afresh.

"You must be mad to interrupt our meeting for such a stupid reason!" one snarled. "Isn't he Snake? How does anyone ever know where a snake is?"

"Only a fool goes looking for a snake!" warned another. "Especially a snake that may well have supernatural powers."

They began to chomp teeth among themselves, revisiting Snake's exploits and attributing his mediatory and mysterious renown to supernatural forces.

Ernest didn't join them. He just looked

coolly at me, the thoughts of his wise young eyes not deigning to trouble the air with a furrow or a frown.

But I suspected he thought like the elders that I was foolish to think I could find Snake just because I wanted to.

I was beginning to think I was foolish, too.

Foolish to go looking for a man who appeared only when he wanted, and disappeared when he felt like.

Foolish to think I was a war journalist and go nosing for stories in war-torn places, when if I tried hard enough I could find my ironies peeking out of a hammock – couldn't I? – at a peaceful beach-side resort, a long Daiquiri at my side.

I felt mightily foolish, for sure, with Ernest training his cool wise eyes on me, and me saying nothing, and me deciding to say something, anything, so as not to appear foolish, and me not knowing what to say, and me deciding to just open my mouth in the hope that some passing pearl of wisdom would decide to twist thereward, cross legs, and chill out on the bench of my lips.

So I opened my mouth.

And the room was rocked by a loud explosion!

Another followed.

The room lit up with the crimson of fire.

Cries and screams!

Cries and screams in the corridor outside!

Cries and screams in the yard outside!

Cries and screams inside – in the room!

In the room!

Feet.

Feet, inside, leaping for the door!

Feet.

Feet rushing in the corridor outside!

Feet.

Feet everywhere, dashing for dear life!

"Dem don come! Dem don come!"

Panic!

Cries!

 Screams!

Everyone whirling in a vortex!

Then the room. Just the room. Empty.

Empty except for Ernest and I.

Me.

Me, frozen by fearful confusion.

Ernest...

Ernest... What about Ernest?

Me, my heart in my throat, pounded up there by pulsing pestles of dread.

Ernest...

Ernest, striding to me cool as ice.

"The first rule of survival is not to panic," says he. He grasps my arm firmly and eases me out of the room.

In the heat of war is the ice of death, is the

ice of dying. I wasn't dead. I wasn't dying. But around me, all around me, was death, was dying.

Was blood.

Blood!

Limbs torn by explosions!

Were roofs.

Roofs sagging under the strange weight of fire.

Fire has weight, you know.

Were walls.

Walls collapsing.

Panic!

Death!

Dying!

And I in ice.

For in the heat is ice. The icy hand of Ernest. The icy coolness of his eyes. The ice in his voice. And the ice of my fear.

And in the ice I knew not how we escaped the theater of war, but I found myself alone in a culvert.

Alone with Ernest.

"This is as safe a place as any," says he.

And a short boom away from the culvert, a short dying away, are the sounds of the unsafe, the sounds of people in death throes, of people in panic, of people at war, of people and fire.

Of fires. Five. Ten. A hundred.

A hundred fires raging. The music in fire, like the cough-coughing of baby thunders, pulsing, pulsing in synchrony with the big guns. Mortars. State-of-the-art mortars.

"Where did they get such big guns?"

I have spoken aloud my thought. A foolish thought. I should be worrying about whether I would live, whether I would live with limbs intact, members in place, but I'm worrying about guns, about the supply source of big guns. It is the heat of war and the ice of fear. It does things to the brain. Always.

Ernest does not answer at first. Then he answers, but he is not answering my question. He says, "The second rule of survival, in this curious kind of war, is to shut everything out. Everything that ravages around."

One beat of silence, then he adds, "Tell me about yourself. About Lagos these days."

What I heave is not a sigh. It is a war kind of noise.

Tell me about yourself…

I am counting the words.

About Lagos these days…

I am counting the words. Weighing them.

And away from the culvert, away from the faeces my nose has weighed to come from some itinerant – probably lunatic – adult of ample girth and robust bowels, deposited no more than five paces to my left in our little tunnel, in the shifting shades, surrounded by the shadows of fear, iced by the full-moon cool of cool Mr

Ernest, I am counting the big booms of the big guns, and weighing the big bushels of the big hatred of brother for brother... in this curious kind of war.

No, I can't talk about myself, I announce silently to the booming corridors of my stock-taking fears.

I can't talk about myself walled in Warri by a culvert, walled from war, walled from Lagos, walled from Lagos by war, Lagos these days...

"Snake," I say aloud to Ernest. "They speak so well of him, but they call him Snake. Can anything good come out of a snake?"

Ernest chuckles.

I can tell he feels he will like this kind of talk. It isn't talk about myself. It isn't talk about Lagos. But it is a shutting out. A shutting out – the second rule of survival in this curious kind of war.

"One of the most wonderful things that ever

happened to me came out of a snake," Ernest is telling me.

There is an explosion a short rat-a-tat away. The blood-light of destruction brightens the culvert, and caught in the light of war, Ernest's face beams hard, steely hard.

The light dies and shadows shade Ernest's face again. In the shadows, how does he look, this strange man of ice?

He looks distinguished, the smile of reminiscence sitting with grace on his face.

He looks very, very distinguished.

He could easily be an acolyte of international diplomacy, waiting for fifteen more maturing years, perhaps, to ease him into the distinction of being the second black man to head the UN.

I stare at him. The man's aura hovers strangely. Hovers between a merciless, steel-hard criminal-type and a responsible, well-bred diplomat-type.

He is strange, this Ernest.

Strange.

And he is talking about snakes.

Is he talking about Snake the man? Was he ever a witness of Snake's legendary diplodazzle?

No, he is not talking about Snake. He is talking about snakes.

"I was appalled to find that Shendam was crawling with snakes," he says.

Shendam. Snakes. What is this?

He glances across at me. "I was once a pastor, you know. A pastor of the Mount Olive Mission which has its headquarters in the US."

"You were once a pastor?" My mouth falls open.

In this war raging through the muzzle of big guns muscled by youths, I see a commander of youths corralled by surprise from his mufti-merry platoon, sequestered by the inevitabilities of war into a tunnel, all curled up, all huddled in, with a story-hungry writer in search of a snake.

I see, when the crimson flashes of war dip right, I see a distinguished-looking fellow, princely cut for the sensitive assignments of diplomatic missions and high-level international service.

I see anything in the man, anything, through the ash and smother of the war-smoke that chokes our hide-out, I see anything but the priestly airs and incense of the soutane.

Nor ever can see it.

For do the things of God cheerily throw themselves up for beholding when the cataract of the devilish deeds of a devilish war rears mountainous across all the eye's horizon?

But Ernest isn't saying he *is* a priest. He is saying he *was* once a priest.

Ernest speaks again and bleeds my logic in one whiplash.

"I suppose you could still call me a pastor,"

he says.

I could still call him a pastor…

Not on your life, soldier boy. Who do you think you are, to think you can fool me. You're a war leader, old boy. Every inch a war leader as I am not a cheerleader with purple pompoms and blonde curls and large dahlia eyes.

"It's just that the mission field has changed," he says. "The sheep are different."

I stare at him across the dancing specks of ash borne on red air streams. I stare at him and let him continue.

"The Mount Olive Mission has a presence in over a hundred countries and I was in South Africa for several years before I was assigned home to Nigeria. To Shendam in Plateau State. When I arrived at the pastor's residence with my son Johnny –"

"You have a son?"

"He was eight years old at the time." The

pause throbs. "I know what you're thinking," he says. "I'm not as young as I look. But even at that, I had him early – too young to marry his mother, who later died of heartbreak. Pastors sometimes have a dark past, you know. But in Christ – in Christ we are born anew. Sometimes I think God delights to make good of bad. It catches man's attention."

He catches his breath, and I'm tempted to say a thing or two, but he begins to speak again and I decide to leave his talk to the sweet freedom of a runaway stream:

The cook and steward and other house and compound staff were all there outside the house waiting to welcome us. It was a lovely day for Johnny and I. We immediately fell in love with the immensely large compound and sprawling colonial-type bungalow. My son takes after me in his love for wide spaces. The pastor's residence of the Mount Olive Mission in

Shendam was a most spacious place. It was all we could have wished for.

So I thought.

Until I beheld a bizarre spectacle the next day.

I had just stepped out to the terrace when I saw two women, wives of compound staff, running for dear life, their hands in the air.

Chasing them were two compound males, machetes in their hands. I was aghast. Was there to be a slaughtering in my premises? There didn't seem to be enough time to prevent it. The men were closing up on the women. I shouted for mercy. "Mercy," I cried. "Mercy!" But the machetes came down.

Struck.

Struck hard.

But not at the women.

At the ground. At the ground short of the women.

At the ground, again and again, short of the women.

What was happening?

Some strange religious ritual?

The men raised their machetes. From the tip of each hung a slain snake.

My compound was filled with snakes.

The revolting creatures seemed to prefer going after the women, but that was no consolation to me. I hadn't been informed that they went *only* after women.

And I had an eight-year-old boy that I loved with my life. How was I to protect him? Books are an awfully useful thing. You learn so much from books. But there are many things that books don't tell you.

Or newspapers either.

No newspaper or book had told me that Shendam was the land of snakes. None had informed me that my compound, the compound

of the resident pastor of the Mount Olive
Mission in Shendam was the hive, the nest, the
very incubator of serpents. You could perhaps
have excused the paucity of information had the
snakes all been harmless. But it wasn't so. Many
were venomous. Some very, very deadly.

***

Ernest sighed. Outside the culvert a war
raged. Inside, a silence. And in the silence I
heard a scrabbling sound. Was it a snake?

No.

Just a cockroach. And a lizard.

The lizard was scurrying after the cockroach.
It caught it. It gobbled it. It did three red-neck
press-ups. Stood there, proud. Was the lizard
going to be caught, too, and gobbled?

By a snake?

The lizard didn't seem frightened. It wasn't
racing for its life. That meant no snake was
nearby. The lizard would know.

Or would it?

I looked around me. One had to be careful. Very careful.

I glanced at Ernest. "I wouldn't stay in a place like that for anything," I told him. "I would pack my bags and vamoose."

"Missionaries are hardly at liberty to leave their posts. The mission field is a hive of trouble and problems. We are called to help bring solutions."

"So what did you do?"

"I prayed."

Silence.

He prayed.

It occurs to me that I have been listening to Ernest with belief. I have believed that he was a missionary, a pastor. This hard man with bones near the surface.

Bones of steel that harden his aura into rock. A pastor, a missionary. This street youth, this gutter youth. And I believe. And look, check out his English. His is the easy language of privileged breeding. Not English boringly and stiltedly learned from English textbooks.

What am I to make of all this?

I go over it. A street-wise, gutter thug. Distinguished. Once a pastor, a missionary. Now a commander of warring youths – he has not told me this, but I know it. He is well-bred. And he prays. Thug. Praying thug.

What am I to make of such contradictions?

"So did the snakes vanish?" I ask him.

"They did. At least most of them."

Pregnant pause.

"So did you just wake up one morning – the next morning – after you prayed – and found that the snakes had disappeared?"

"I first had to get pigs."

"Pigs?"

"Yes. Pigs. I filled the compound with pigs. I

discovered that pigs are rather known to relish snakes. They belch them down with a speed and a grunt Johnny would be hard pressed to muster over his favorite ice cream." He hesitates. "You didn't know that, did you?"

"I guess not."

"Books don't say everything. Nor newspapers. I have a high regard for both, I assure you. A very high regard. But they don't tell you for instance that some of our countrymen sail the China seas – as pirates."

"'Scuse me. What did you say?"

Ernest chuckles. "Let's leave that for the time being."

"Especially since we are supposed to be laundering our image," I quip. But I'm intrigued and resolve to make Ernest come back to this titbit later.

Ernest doesn't speak for a long moment and I wonder what's going through his mind. Then he says, "I was telling you how great good came out of a snake for me."

"Yes," I reply, "but the pigs gobbled up all the snakes and all the great good and you lived sorrowfully ever after."

"Not quite," he laughs. "But, yes, I suppose you could say there was another problem. It was my son Johnny. Johnny and the compound kids. The bush compound kids. The children of the cook and steward and groundsmen."

Bush? I hadn't known the man hunched over in the darkened tunnel for any length of time, but I had pieced together a certain impression of him, howbeit mottled. But what he was saying now was thoroughly out of character.

Bush...

I squint through the pall of black smoke some terrorist breeze has just exploded on us.

"It occurs to me that you're of privileged birth," I tell him delicately, then not so delicately

107

I add, "which is rather incongruous, seeing there is a streetwise streak to you, a steel-hardness."

I'm getting poised now to wrestle him to the ground on the *bush* bit, but his laughter smashes in, flattening me to the canvas. "My father was a Supreme Court judge. We were privileged all right. Private schools and all that."

That figured. Upper-crust breeding. But the low-life hardness – where did it come from?

I didn't ask him that though, I just said, "So your blue birth made you a snob?"

"I suppose you could say that. I couldn't bear to see my blue-eyed Johnny, black as he was, mucking around with black-eyed beans, blue as they tried to be. But this bothered me. I was a pastor, remember. A pastor. I was supposed to have equal regard for all, but here I was, esteeming my son Johnny and despising his playmates."

I shake my head. "Just because they

belonged to a different class."

"Different?" my culvert companion snorts. "More like lower, in my judgment. A decidedly lower class."

"Snob!"

Ernest laughs. "But it wasn't a laughing matter," he says. "I was dead serious about my prejudice. I forbade Johnny to play with the kids. And at supper on the evening of my Nazi order, a most uncomfortable conversation ensued between my boy and me."

A speck of ash floats across on proud gray sails. It is strong. Like a youth in arrogant prime. Suddenly it does a purler, taken captive by culvert gravity.

And I, a culvert captive, listen raptly to the conversation Ernest replays.

"But Dad, what did they do wrong? Why don't you want me to play with them?"

"Can't you see?"

"See what, Dad?"

"They are dirty! They play in the sun and stink and are dirty!"

"But Dad, when I play in the sun, I stink, too, and am dirty."

"It's not the same."

"Dad, do they really stink? I never smell them."

"See how they go around – in underpants! They don't even have the decency to wear shorts. If they can't afford shirts, surely they can afford shorts."

"Dad, may I give them some of my clothes? I've got more than I can wear." Pause. "Well, Dad, if you don't want me to give them the new ones, what about the old ones I never use?"

In the darkling culvert, in the shower of ash from war and burning, hounded by outside cries of horror, Ernest groans. Not for the war outside. Not about the war outside. But for the war within. Always the worst of wars. The war within. Always the cause of the wars outside.

"I just stared speechlessly at my boy," he says. "The little lad just didn't understand. And I didn't know how to explain it to him. How do you explain prejudice? How do you tell a little boy that prejudice is a good thing when you know it is evil? How do you tell a little boy his innocence is convicting you, is churning up your unrighteousness, bringing out your devils? Well, I wasn't prepared to confront my devils and ponder the smirch in my dog collar. I put my foot down. Placed it firmly on swastika tiles: No more mucking about with the bush compound kids."

Ernest exhales. "Johnny was a good lad and he tried to obey me. But good people have never found it easy obeying bad laws. Johnny certainly didn't. Especially over Jonathan. Jonathan was the oldest of the compound kids. He was nine. I should have named Johnny David. For he and Jonathan were inseparable. They tried to keep their David and Jonathan camaraderie from me, but if they had succeeded it would not have been a true David and Jonathan bond. And it was. I hated Jonathan. Hated him. Hated him with ear-reddening hatred. No, it wasn't just because Jonathan made Johnny break my order repeatedly. No. It was because Jonathan was not in the frying pan of my prejudice. He was in the very fire. *The very fire.*

"You see, Jonathan was not an indigene of Shendam. He came from – of all places – my state. But his tribe and mine were traditional enemies – even though our penchant is legendary for taking each other's sisters as wives. And it was this Jonathan, this Jonathan from the wrong tribe, from the hated tribe, that of all the Jonathans in Shendam, of all the Jonathans in the world, Johnny chose to be

David to. I burned inside. I would never allow it. No. Not ever.

"But I had to be careful. It would be foolish to let the running pus hidden by my dog collar escape and spread its blotch all over my cassock for the world to see. The pastor of the respected Mount Olive Mission – no more than a hate-filled bigot? No, I had to be cunning and do my utmost to hide the buzzard wings of my secret sin. But this was not to be. For the very next day my iniquity screeched aloft to rake the eye.

"I was in the living room immersed in private Bible study when I heard furtive whisperings coming from the pantry. I put down my Bible and tiptoed to the pantry. There, in a corner, were Johnny and Jonathan leafing happily through the story of – guess – David and Jonathan in a comic book. I stormed at them and tore the comic from their hands. Unbridled blows rocked my fists and Jonathan barely escaped with his life. I was livid. It was one thing to have my son playing with the rascal outside, it was quite another to have the ragamuffin inside soiling the tiles of my squeaky-clean floor."

There were furrows now in the face of Ice-E.

So Mr Cool could lose his cool?

"And Johnny," I interjected. "How did he take it? How did he take this child battery from a pastor father?"

"Oh Johnny, Johnny... He sulked for days and would barely eat. Then one evening he said something that made me resolve to shift my tactics to different gear. We were having dinner. Well, I was having, and I was trying to coax him into doing the same. He looked up from his plate and stared at me with convicting eyes. 'Dad, you're a hypocrite,' he said. 'You're not practicing what you preach. Remember what you preached on Sunday?'

"A shiver ran through me. What had I preached on Sunday? As I pondered, a chunk of my sermon came trundling down reluctant byways –

"I was in South Africa for several years. A land that had not too long ago been ruled by white people. You should see how the whites still treat the blacks. Some of their churches are still all-white. They do everything to keep black people away. If you stray in and take a seat, the entire pew would be abandoned by the whites. You'd find yourself shamefully alone in a whole pew. They would rather stand than share a pew with you. Yet they read the Bible and profess to be Christians. But they're just Pharisees – hypocrites!

"*Pharisees! Hypocrites! Pharisees! Hypocrites!* The words slammed through my ears like a wedge hammering through the under-slit of a door. Caponté, there is a question I should like to ask you –"

I tingled, delightfully surprised that Ernest knew my name. I couldn't remember the spokesman of our party mentioning it. "Did you just call my name?"

Ernest grinned. "Don't you think I read papers? Your column, Caponté, is a great favorite of mine. I think one day I should like to write short-story columns myself. I do have a pretty tale or two to tell."

"I should imagine so," I muttered, thinking of the mesmerizing story he was now telling.

"So some of the Christian folks in South Africa are hypocrites," Ernest clawed back in. "And because they're white people rubbing their prejudices in black faces, we call them racists and despise them with that peculiar venom reserved for racists. The venom that destroys not only the vessel it is poured into, but its own holding calabash. The question I would like to ask is this: Is the poison everyone plays around with, when the prejudice rubbed is from black hand to black face – is the poison any less mutually destructive?

"Hypocrite, my little Johnny had called me, his understanding soaring on wings beyond his years, on wings assuredly heaven-sent. *Hypocrite.* Listen, Caponté, my little boy was telling the truth. He was. So I decided that I would change. I would change. Ah, but not my prejudices. No, not my prejudices at all. I would change my tactics on Johnny – that's what I would change. And I would make Johnny change. That's what had to change – Johnny. I would devise a new way to make Johnny fall in line with me, in line with my prejudices, my predilections of years, of birth, born of a culture that clutches its traditions closely to its breast like an external heart.

"This was the path of safety. Truth was good

and Johnny was telling it. I liked it. I was raising my boy right. But this was one truth that would have to bide its time and wait for the reinforcement of circumstances and event to mature it into an earthmover that could dislodge the heart of centuries – and winkle out my little prejudice.

"I decided that getting Johnny to live for a while with an upper-crust family would help matters nicely along. He would see, in a way that he could never see from the pulpit of a reverend gentleman's abode, that humankind, like all of nature, observes the laws of status and stratification. I knew of the right family."

Another pall of black smoke had drifted into the culvert. I couldn't see Ernest's face, but I sensed he was turning to me. "You know Golden Boy? Golden Boy of Plateau?"

I grunted a yes. Not because I like to lie, but because people think writers should know everything. Especially writers of popular columns.

"The bulk of Golden Boy's wealth comes from his businesses in South Africa," Ernest informed me. "We had met there and struck up an excellent friendship."

A sudden blaze of crimson surprised the black pall and caught the glint in Ernest's eyes. Was the glint there because Ernest had enjoyed Golden Boy's largess? Or was it there because he knew I was lying when I pretended to know Golden Boy? That was the thing about war. You found yourself worrying about trivia.

"Without letting Johnny know what I had in mind," Ernest went on, "I made arrangements the very next day and took Johnny straight from school to Golden Boy's little palace in the suburbs of Jos. Two days later, as I was studying my Bible at home in the living room, all alone, the house staff having gone for siesta, I fell into a deep slumber. I don't know what woke me, but I opened my eyes to find myself staring into the eyes of a snake. It was a snake of the most venomous sort. And a muscular beast to boot. It was staring at me, slithering to me.

"A snake. One I knew to be deadly. So deadly. The deadliest of the Shendam serpents. Its fangs spelled instant death. And it was close. So close. So close that I feared that if I as much as batted an eyelid, it would lunge and strike and I would be dead. Then something else came into my vision. Jonathan. Jonathan with his face still swollen and bruised from my battering. He slipped into the room and immediately slipped out when he saw me. Later he explained that having not seen a trace of Johnny for two days he decided to risk my thunder to see if his soul-mate was ill or in chains in a dungeon or something.

"Jonathan! Why had he slipped out? *Why?*

Hadn't he seen the snake? Hadn't he understood my predicament? *Hadn't he?* I do not think anyone could ever call me a coward. I have lived a hard and reckless life. I have seen death more times than a cat in a pit bull kennel – and laughed in the face of it. But that was before Jesus arrested me. With this arrest and the working of His Holy Spirit in me had come a tenderness, howbeit flawed as shown in my treatment of Jonathan and the other compound kids. Was it this tenderness that was now rendering me helpless in the cold gaze of the snake? Or was it my cruelty to Jonathan and the kids?

"I didn't want to die. I had Johnny to think of. I was a praying man, but in the winkless eyes of the snake I could find no prayer. All I could think of was Jonathan. Why had he left? *Why?* What I expected him to do had he stayed, I know not, but I was grieved to death that he had left.

The snake inched closer. Any moment now…

"I clamped my eyes shut. I had given up. I was going to die. But I didn't want to die locked in the eyes of this huge, slithering coil of evil. I wanted to think of my beloved Johnny, to see his face, his laughter, his joys, his successes, the beauty of the things I had lined out for him but would now never give, and then I saw, I saw that no man had anything real, anything of true value, to give anyone but the love of Christ. And I saw that Jonathan was the love of Christ to Johnny. And I had shut the door. Had shut from Johnny the only true gift I could have given him. *Had shut the door.*

"I opened it now. Opened my eyes. For I had heard a sound. A sound that snakes don't make. And there before me stood Jonathan, his face still carrying my battering. One hand held the snake by its head, keeping its mouth closed. The other had it by the tail. The beast struggled robustly, for it was of muscular size and very much alive. Jonathan was sweating stone drops. And I was leaping up, was springing up, galvanized into action by this boy, the courage of this boy, this little boy from the wrong tribe, the hated tribe.

"'Hold it tight,' I cried. 'Don't let go!' I bounded into the kitchen and returned with a butcher's knife. A swipe. And the beast was dead. Later Jonathan said he had only slipped out of the room to find something good to attack the snake with. Not seeing any, he returned to use his hands."

In our little tunnel, hidden from war outside, I stare at Ernest and the question gushes out of its own accord: "And where is Jonathan today?"

"He is with Johnny abroad. They are at Eton. Jonathan is my son now. I adopted him and his three siblings. And I have seven other adopted children, all from the wrong tribes, and I love them like my very own flesh. For now my heart lives out what my head has always known: all humankind is created for love, created to be loved. This is what Christ has done for me..."

"Out of a snake..."

"Yes," Ernest replies. "Out of a snake."

We fall silent, and I'm thinking many things. I'm thinking that this is one of the most beautiful stories my roving life has yet uncovered, and it all came out here in a culvert. In the shadows. With war raging outside. War amongst brothers. Brothers across a divide, a divide erected by the foolish traditions of men, traditions that lie and say of brothers, "They are of the wrong tribe. Hate them."

But this man listened to the truth, to the truth that came out of a snake, out of an unlikely place...

And I am listening...

I am listening in the shadows, in the stillness

of a culvert, I am listening to the thoughts that would take a lifetime to plumb, for we all have our prejudices, our little prejudices.

We call them little, but their consequences are dire.

Little prejudices. Big wars.

Little prejudices. Big sufferings.

Little prejudices. Big dyings.

Big dyings. Big dyings. Big dyings. For no death is little.

I would need a lifetime…

Or maybe just a moment.

The little moment it takes to hear a story in a culvert, a war raging outside.

Inside, a quiet. Then a voice breaks the quiet. Ernest says, "Time to go."

Time to go? To go where? Into war?

Ernest says, "I only came here to rest. And to tell you a story dear to me, a story I hope will be cherished all the days of our little lives."

He scoots over to me and nudges me out of the tunnel. The light outside is harsh to my eyes, the air acrid. He grasps my arm and takes me into the theater of war. And I, a sheep, follow.

"When I am done with the mission field of the sword," Ernest says, "I shall move into the mission field of the pen – a greater commission. I have seen things. Things that should be said."

He frowns in thought. "I shall start, perhaps, with my days on the China seas... my days of piracy."

The China seas... Piracy...

"Do you know I was once a pirate?"

Silence.

Is he expecting me to lie like I did about knowing Golden Boy? Trivia in war.

Step.

We have just taken another step into the theater of war, I, a sheep, following.

"My incorruptible Supreme Court judge of a

father, sadly did not restrict his iron-strict temper to the courts of law but brandished it everywhere. I fled from home. I was only fifteen. I wound up fleeing ships, shouting jeers; ships we had plundered, pillaged."

His low-life steeliness. It figured. It figured now, as everything in time does.

Step.

I, a sheep, following.

"We plundered all the way to China. In China I got a special tattoo."

He sweeps up his sleeve. I see the tattoo. The tattoo they said marked him out. Then he whips out the mask he uses. It comes as no surprise to me. I had suspected it earlier, as you probably did.

No, I had known it. I knew it, therefore I, a sheep, stepped with Snake into the theater of war.

Snake.

They had not exaggerated his prowess. No, they had not said the half of it. They had called it magical, but this wasn't magic. It was simply God working through man. Showing man He is there, always there.

Always there, even in the worst scenarios of the consequences of man's many foolishnesses...

There, even in the most supreme heights, the most abject nadir, of man's arrogant attempts to dis-equate God from life...

From life, our lives, His Life.

He is there, God is there, always there, for any who will hearken, who will come to Him.

Let him who has ears hear.

And Warri burned needlessly.

About the Author

PHILIP BEGHO is the author of several award-winning books. His wide-ranging interest has seen him in a varied career that has spanned journalism, banking, business, legal practice and university teaching. He has also engaged in film and theatrical production.

He now works as a full-time writer, concentrating largely on children's literature and verse drama.